ADVENTURES AT HOUND HOTEL

Raintree is an imprint of Capstone Global Library Limited, a company incorporated in
England and Wales having its registered office at 7 Pilgrim Street, London, EC4V 6LB –
Registered company number: 6695582

www.raintree.co.uk
myorders@raintree.co.uk

Edited by Clare Lewis and Julie Gassman
Designed by Russell Griesmer
Original illustrations © Capstone Global Library Limited 2015
Illustrated by Deborah Melmon
Production by Charmaine Whitman
Originated by Capstone Global Library
Printed and bound in China.

ISBN 978-1-4062-9229-9 (paperback)
18 17 16 15 14
10 9 8 7 6 5 4 3 2 1

British Library Cataloguing in Publication Data
A full catalogue record for this book is available from
the British Library.

Mudball Molly

by Shelley Swanson Sateren

illustrated by Deborah Melmon

CONTENTS

ADVENTURES AT HOUND HOTEL

IT'S TIME FOR YOUR ADVENTURE AT HOUND HOTEL!

At Hound Hotel, dogs are given the royal treatment. We are a top-notch boarding kennel. When your dog stays with us, we will follow your feeding schedule, take them for walks and tuck them into bed at night.

We are just a short walk away from the dogs — the kennels are located in a heated building at the end of our driveway. Every dog has his or her own kennel, with a bed, blanket and water bowl.

Rest assured … a stay at the Hound Hotel is like a holiday for your dog. We have a large playground, plenty of toys and a pool for the dogs to play in, in the summer. Your dog will love playing with the other guests.

HOUND HOTEL
WHO'S WHO

WINIFRED WOLFE

Hound Hotel is run by Winifred Wolfe, a lifelong dog lover. Winifred loves all types of dogs. She likes to get to know every breed. When she's not taking care of the canines, she writes books about – that's right – dogs.

ALFIE AND ALFREEDA WOLFE

Winifred's twins help out as much as they can. Whether your dog needs gentle attention or extra playtime, Alfreeda and Alfie provide special services you can't find anywhere else. Your dog will never get bored whilst these two are helping out.

WOLFGANG WOLFE

Winifred's husband helps out at the hotel whenever he can, but he spends most of his time travelling to study packs of wolves. Wolfgang is a real wolf lover – he even named his children after pack leaders, the alpha wolves. Every wolf pack has two alpha wolves: a male wolf and a female wolf, just like the Wolfe family twins.

Next time your family goes on holiday, bring your dog to Hound Hotel.

Your pooch is sure to have a howling good time!

CHAPTER 1
Complete shaggy mess

I'm Alfie Wolfe, and there's one thing I hate. Getting groomed! *Ugh*!

I hate having my hair cut or even brushed. And getting dirt and gunk cleaned out of my ears and fingernails? Yuck.

I really hate getting it done properly by my mum. It hurts, it's boring and it takes forever. It's the most horrible thing ever!

A few weeks ago, I met a dog that hated being groomed even more than I do, if you can believe that. Her name was Molly. Molly the West Highland white terrier.

White? Ha! Not even close. When I first met her, she didn't even look like a Westie. (That's the nickname for that kind of terrier.)

Westies are pure white after they've been washed. But Molly wouldn't go anywhere near the bath, so she was the colour of mud.

She wouldn't let anyone near her with a hairbrush or scissors. So she was a complete shaggy mess too. I couldn't even see her eyes.

I'll tell you the whole story

about Molly the little mudball. Perhaps you're saying, "Who cares? So what if a dog doesn't want to get her hair washed or cut? Who does?"

Well, it turned out that somebody had a lot to lose if Molly didn't get groomed like a show dog.

That somebody was *me*.

🐾 🐾 🐾

It all started on a Friday. The day had started out quite normally. At about seven o'clock, I hit my dog-shaped alarm clock to make it stop barking.

I leapt out of bed and hurried to get ready for school. I had to beat my sister, Alfreeda. She makes everything into a competition. You see, she always acts like the alpha child in our house. Top dog in every way. The fastest. The cleverest. The strongest. The bravest. It drives me mad!

But on that day I had beaten her in two departments: dressing and grooming.

At alpha-boy speed, I grabbed my jeans and a Hound Hotel T-shirt off of my floor and pulled them on. I dashed to the bathroom and bumped Alfreeda away from the mirror.

"Hey, stop it!" she screamed.

Before she had a chance to shove me back, I rubbed my teeth with a finger of toothpaste. I gave them one good rub. Then I ran my fingers through my hair. Just one quick flick is all it took.

"Finished," I said and jumped to the doorway. "Beat you!"

Alfreeda rolled her eyes.

"Alfie," she said in her tired-teacher voice. "When will you ever understand? Mum will just make you do it again. Or she'll take over and do it, as you're so helpless. Just like she always does."

I crossed my eyeballs at Alfreeda. "Doubt it," I said.

"Don't doubt it," she said.

Suddenly I saw two sisters standing in front of me. No one needs two sisters! So I uncrossed my eyeballs and flew downstairs.

In about four seconds flat, I poured a bowl of cereal and raced to the kennel building. It's at the end of our long driveway, past the apple trees and chicken coop.

I wolfed down my breakfast on the way. I don't waste time with spoons, not when I can be playing with dogs down at the kennels. And I only got a little bit of milk on my T-shirt. Okay, a lot.

I threw open the office door and shouted, "Mum! I'm up and ready!"

"Oh, good. Come here, Alfie," she called from down the hallway. Her voice sounded even more cheerful than normal.

I walked through the office, past the utility room, and past the storeroom. She was all the way at the back of the building, in the grooming room.

The grooming room has a table that moves up and down, depending on the size of the dog. We have a huge bath. Next to the bath is a shelf full of all sorts of dog shampoos and lots of Hound Hotel towels.

And then there are the grooming tools. Mum adds her finishing touches with shavers, clippers and hair-driers.

"Is the Westie here yet?" I asked.

"No," Mum said and smiled at me. "Molly will be here when you get back from school."

"Have any other dogs checked in?" I asked.

"Not yet. More are coming later on, around dinnertime." Mum patted the dog-grooming table. "Hop up, Alfie."

I groaned, long and *loud*. "Not today, Mum," I said. "You always do this to me."

"Well, sweetheart, today it's even more important that you look your very best," she said in a voice that sounded like a bird singing in springtime. It made me very suspicious.

So I twisted around and sprinted out of the door.

CHAPTER 2
Good enough!

"Not so fast, Mr," Mum said. She grabbed my arm. Gentle, but firm.

Mum's got some strong muscles. She's lugged around a lot of big dogs for an awful lot of years. She's always lifting them in and out of the bath and on and off of the grooming table.

She picked me up and popped me onto the table, like I weighed no more than a tiny Chihuahua.

Mum grabbed a dog brush. It was the big kind that can handle big grooming jobs on big furry dogs. The brush had my name on it. Mum always used it on my fur.

She started to pull through my mop of hair. To be honest, I've got poodle-like hair. (Alfreeda has too.) It's really thick and curly and crazy. Combs don't work. Really, only dog brushes can do the job.

"Please, Mum." I groaned again. "It's Friday. Even the teachers dress down on Fridays. Who cares what I look like?"

"Calm down, Alfie," Mum said. She pulled a dead ladybird out of my hair. She dropped it next to the little piles of sticky-weed she'd already pulled out.

Then she started to brush. And brush. Then she brushed a bit more.

She wouldn't stop! She was going completely overboard!

"That's good enough," I complained. "Stop!"

"Relax, Alfie," Mum said. At last, she put the brush down onto the table. But then she grabbed some scissors.

"No!" I cried. "I don't need a haircut!"

"Alfie, you haven't looked this shaggy in months," she said. "Now sit still, please, so I can do this properly."

I knew what that meant. *Properly* meant *perfectly.* You see, my mum is a professional dog groomer. The best there is. She always made our hotel guests look fantastic before they went home. She was famous for it.

Sometimes I think Mum forgets I'm a child and not a canine. I wasn't supposed to look perfect.

Now I couldn't wiggle or anything. Not with scissors pointed at my head. I sighed loudly.

"This is the worst part," I said. "Sitting still, forever and ever. How long is this going to take?"

Mum smiled. Then she said in that sing-song, springtime robin voice, "If you miss the school bus, I'll drive you to school."

"Why?" I cried. "Mum, why is it so important that I get my hair cut right now?"

"Well, sweetheart," she said in a very sweet voice, "you know my friend from school, Primrose? Her family runs the food shop in town?"

"Yes," I said. "The world's tiniest grown-up. She can't pat me on the head anymore. I'm as tall as her now. What about her?"

"She's getting married tomorrow," Mum

said. "In her parents' garden. Isn't that exciting?"

"No," I said. "So what?"

"Well," Mum cleared her throat and continued, "Primrose and her husband-to-be, Harry, adopted a little Westie called Molly two months ago. Primrose wants Molly to be the flower girl at her wedding. Isn't that sweet?"

"No," I said.

Mum chewed her lip and started to trim my fringe.

"Get to the point, Mum," I said.

"Okay, Alfie!" Mum snapped and chopped off half my fringe. I looked around the room. Wow, I could see things with my left eyeball. Nice and clearly. Not like I was looking through a dirty curtain anymore.

"Let me explain," Mum said. "You see, Molly won't let anyone groom her. Not Primrose, not Harry, no one. Primrose says I'm her one and only hope. She wants Molly looking like a Westie show dog in time for the wedding tomorrow. The wedding starts at two o'clock. But Molly should look like a show dog for the rehearsal tonight. At the very latest, she needs to be ready for photos at ten tomorrow."

"What's that got to do with me?" I asked.

"Well, you see, Alfie," Mum went on, clipping away at my hair, "it sounds like Molly is frightened of being groomed. She's young – she's only about three years old. Perhaps her first owner didn't groom her, so Molly's afraid of being groomed now. Or perhaps the owner was too rough with Molly while she brushed and bathed her. Who knows?"

"And the point is?" I asked.

"Calm down, Alfie," Mum said. "I told Primrose I'd try to groom Molly beautifully by tomorrow. But I said I didn't have high hopes. It can take weeks of slow, calm, gentle training to turn a dog's grooming fears around. I explained to Primrose that she needs a back-up plan for her flower girl. So…"

"Yes?" I said.

"Well, Alfie," Mum said, "I offered your services to Primrose. As a back-up page boy."

"What?" I screamed and leapt off of the grooming table.

CHAPTER 3
Half a haircut

I shot out of the kennel building and up our driveway, all the way out to the country lane. That's where the school bus picks up Alfreeda and me.

I climbed up the trunk of an old tree. I wriggled up to a high branch and held on tight.

Mum's a fast runner. She's built up powerful legs over the years, chasing after runaway dogs.

She peered up
the tree trunk.

"Alfie, come
down," she said.
"Please listen."

"No," I said. "I
don't want to be a
page boy or a flower
dog or anything! Let
her do it!" I pointed
at Alfreeda.

She walked over with
her rucksack on, ready
for school. "Let me do
what?" she asked.

Then she looked
at me and started to
laugh her head off.

"What have you done to your hair?" she cried. "Wow! I'd hide in a tree too.

Slowly, I reached up and rubbed my fingers over my head, the whole top of it.

A thick furry helmet covered half of my head. The other side was cropped short against my head, from the top of my forehead to the back of my neck.

My heart started to pound.

Alfreeda looked at Mum. "What's he talking about?" she asked. "Let me do what?"

Mum quickly explained the problem.

"Why did you say Alfie would do it?" Alfreeda cried. "Why not me? I would have so much fun, throwing flower petals all over the place. Everyone would take photos of me. I'd be able to eat all that wedding cake. Why didn't you tell Primrose I'd do it?"

"Because Primrose is so tiny," Mum said. "The flower girl or page boy can't be taller than she is. But she doesn't know any little children, except Alfie."

"I'm *not* little, Mum!" I shouted.

"Yeah!" Alfreeda cried. "We're the same height!"

"So why me?" I shouted. "I hate weddings! And why do you always make me get my hair cut? Why not her? She crawls around in the fields and chases after dogs as much as I do. She gets sticky-weed and dead insects in her hair. Why do you only groom me, eh?"

Mum didn't have a chance to answer.

"Because, Alfie," Alfreeda said, "I brush my hair twice a day. *And* I do a top job every time. You never do."

She had a point.

I stared at my sister and realized something: she looked as groomed as a show dog. She had big, puffy, perfect hair, loaded with ribbons. Not a dead insect in sight. Her face and hands and fingernails had a soap-and-water shine. Even her teeth sparkled.

How does she do that? I wondered. *Without help from Mum or anything?* Suddenly I realized my sister was alpha girl in the grooming department.

That's fine, I thought. *Let her have the honour.*

"Okay, kids," Mum said. "These are my thoughts ... Alfreeda, you have big tall hair. It adds inches to your height. Also, you have a very nice habit of standing up straight."

"Thanks, Mum," Alfreeda said.

Mum looked at me. "But you, Alfie?" she said. "You always walk around with your shoulders caved in, sagging towards the ground."

She paused and slouched to show me how I walk. "No matter how many times I tell you to stand up straight, you don't," Mum said. "I can count on you. I know you'll slouch at Primrose's wedding. You won't outsize the bride."

Suddenly, Alfreeda's shoulders caved in. She put her hands on top of her head and squashed her hair flat.

"Please, Mum?" Alfreeda begged. "Tell Primrose I'll do it. If I'm their flower girl, I'm sure they'll let me have seconds at cake time."

"Good plan!" I cried. I leapt out of the tree and landed on the grass with a thud.

I patted my sister on the shoulder then jumped in front of Mum. I stretched my spine out. I stretched my neck as far as it could reach, too. I even stood on my tiptoes. My nose almost touched Mum's nose.

"Sorry, Alfie." She shook her head. "I know that the moment you walk down that garden path, scattering rose petals, you'll forget all about standing up straight. It's settled, Alfie. I'll try, but I doubt Molly will let me groom her. So, you're the back-up page boy. Just take a deep breath. It'll be over before you know it."

"*Aarghhh!*" I fumed. Sometimes it was just useless arguing with my mum!

"It's not fair," Alfreeda complained. "I bet they'll give Alfie thirds at cake time."

Suddenly the school bus roared up.

I dragged my feet up the bus steps behind Alfreeda.

The bus was full of children. They were

talking really loudly, like they always did. But the second I stepped inside, everybody went quiet.

Straight away, fingers started to point at my head. A sea of mouths fell open and started roaring with laughter.

I turned around and jumped off the bus.

CHAPTER 4
Who's this film star?

Mum made me really late for school that morning.

At about eleven o'clock, she finally finished the grooming job.

I was completely groomed, from the top of my head down to my toenails. Even my teeth sparkled.

She made me put on a clean Hound Hotel T-shirt too.

"There, handsome," she said and grinned at me. "We. Are. Done. You look like a prize-winning show dog. All that's missing is the white shirt, trousers and tie."

I was so disgusted, I couldn't even talk.

Mum drove me to school and kept saying, "So handsome! Who knew?"

She parked outside the school and said, "Now, Alfie, stay clean at break time and all afternoon. Tonight, after the groom's dinner, the wedding party is going to rehearse the wedding, in Primrose's parents' rose garden. That means you too."

She had to be joking. I couldn't stay clean for that long! I slammed the car door shut and didn't even say goodbye.

I headed straight into my classroom and my teacher didn't even recognize me.

"Well, who's this film star?" Ms Ruff whispered to me.

I think some of the other children heard her. Everybody stared at me. My friends looked at me with sad faces and said, "Sorry, Alf."

I ran to my desk and wished I could wear a hat at school to cover my hair.

At that moment, I made a rock-solid decision: I would *never* again, in my *whole* life, let *anybody* groom me. Definitely *not* my mum!

Now I knew exactly how that little terrier Molly felt. *My mum had better not force her to get groomed*, I thought. *No dog should have to suffer like this.*

Suddenly, I made another firm decision: I'd make sure that Alfreeda would get the flower-girl job. And I knew exactly how to do it.

*** *** ***

I told Alfreeda my plan on the bus journey home. We shook hands on it.

We got off of the bus and saw a tiny yellow car parked in our driveway. "That must be Primrose's car," Alfreeda said.

"Makes sense," I said. "Let's go."

We raced inside and upstairs to the attic. We dug through boxes and piles of rubbish, searching for the things we needed.

Alfreeda grabbed a straw hat covered in fake flowers out of the fancy-dress box. "Perfect," she said.

She dropped it onto the floor and jumped on it about ten times to flatten it. Then she put it on her head. Dead-looking flowers hung over the rim. A couple of long ribbons hung down on either side too.

Alfreeda tied the ribbons tightly under her chin. The hat squashed her hair flat.

"Perfect!" I said. "How about this?"

I grabbed a tall top hat from the box and put it on.

"Wow," Alfreeda said. "You look almost as tall as Dad!"

Then I stuck my feet into some man-size smart shoes. They had thick heels.

"Cool!" Alfreeda said. "Now you tower over me! Don't forget to stand up really straight when Primrose gets here."

"Okay," I said. "And don't forget to slump your shoulders down."

"I won't." She flew down the attic stairs. About two seconds later, I heard the kitchen door bang shut.

I'm proud to say I tripped only four times on the stairs. We've got a lot of stairs in our big old farmhouse.

Finally I emerged from the house and dragged those boat-size shoes towards the kennel building.

I made it halfway there when the hairiest

man I have ever seen came out of the office door. A furry rocket blasted around him. It flew down the front steps and shot straight towards me.

"Molly!" the man called. "Come back!"

The furry mudball barked her shaggy head off at me. It sounded like this: *errr-RWOW! Errr-RWOW!*

Molly sprang up and dug her long toenails into my ribs. I fell backwards. My shoes and hat flew off. I landed on my bottom in the middle of the driveway.

"Alfie!" the man cried. "You are Alfie, aren't you? The reserve page boy? I was justs coming to find you. Are you okay?"

"I don't know." I groaned.

CHAPTER 5
It's a deal

I sat up, nice and slowly, and checked a few of my bones.

Nothing seemed to be broken. "I think I'm fine," I said. "I'm used to rowdy dogs."

Molly wagged her tail like mad and tried to lick my face. Usually, I don't mind that. But I pushed Molly away. She had really bad breath.

"Goodness, you need to brush your teeth," I said. "*Ugh.*"

She hopped away and climbed inside the top hat, as though it was a rabbit hole or something.

The hairy man grabbed my hand and helped me up. Even his hands were hairy.

He had long, shaggy hair and a bushy beard. He was even hairier than my dad when he gets back from a long wolf-research trip in the wilderness. (That's my dad's job. He's away a lot, studying wolf packs in Canada.)

The strange thing was that the hairy man wore a very smart suit.

He shook my hand and said, "I'm Harry."

"I can see that," I said.

He threw back his head and laughed. "Everyone makes that mistake," he said. "My *name* is Harry. H-A-R-R-Y."

"Oh." I laughed. "I get it! Look, Harry, are you the man who's marrying Primrose? Because I really don't want to be a page boy."

"I thought not," he said. "It was nice of you to offer, though."

"I didn't!" I said. "My mum did."

"*Hmm.*" He rubbed his bushy chin. "The truth is, I hate getting my hair and beard cut, too. Primrose has begged and begged me to get them trimmed before the wedding. But I'm hoping that, if Molly gets groomed, Primrose will be so happy, she'll forget about shaggy old me. Can I strike a deal with you, Alfie my man?"

"Of course," I said. "What is it?"

"If you help your mum make Molly look like a true Westie, I'll give you twenty pounds."

"Wow!" I said and whistled.

"Here's the catch," Harry said. "You have to make sure that Molly's neck and beard are trimmed short."

"Why?" I asked.

"So this will show!" He pulled a skinny dog collar out of his suit-coat pocket. It had tiny yellow roses on it. Two shiny gold rings hung from it. "Our wedding rings!"

Then Harry whistled with his fingers and Molly ran over.

He pulled her shaggy hair away from her neck and put the collar on. As he buckled the collar, he explained.

"You see, Alfie," he said, "Molly will be the flower girl *and* the ring bearer at our wedding tomorrow."

"The ring what-er?" I asked.

"The ring bearer. That means she'll carry the rings to Primrose and me during the wedding ceremony," he said. "I'll whistle, she'll come running, and Primrose will be so surprised to see the beautiful rings on Molly's neck."

"Fantastic," I said. "Don't worry. I won't tell anybody. It'll be a great surprise."

Harry grinned. "So, my friend, can you finish Molly's grooming in time for the rehearsal dinner?"

"Of course," I said, and we shook on it. *For twenty pounds?* I thought. *No problem!*

"Wonderful." Harry started to search in his suit pockets. "I'll even pay you up front. Now, where did I put my wallet?"

He checked and double-checked all of his pockets. Then he triple checked, and his eyes began to bulge out of their sockets – he looked terrified.

Just then Molly ran off. She bolted down the driveway, chasing a couple of robins.

Harry started to shout, "Where's my wallet? Where did I leave it this time? I put all the money for the groom's dinner in it. The dinner starts in half an hour! Where on earth is my money? Oh, no!"

He dashed to the office door, threw it open, and called for Primrose.

She ran outside, and they had a speedy, whispered discussion. Just then I realized that Primrose actually looked like the flower she was named after. She wore a yellow flowery dress and a matching hat.

"Your wallet?" she cried. "You've lost your wallet. Oh, Harry, not again! We have to find it!"

They ran to the little yellow car and jumped inside. Harry started the engine.

"We'll see you at the rehearsal," Primrose called to Mum. "I can't wait to see my Molly looking beautiful. If anything can cheer me up, that will!"

With that, the tiny car sped away.

CHAPTER 6
Backed into a corner

Mum looked at her watch. "It's hopeless, kids," she said. "I can't groom Molly in less than three hours."

"Of course you can't," Alfreeda said. "Please, will you ask Primrose if I can be the flower girl?"

I grabbed Mum's arm and pulled her inside the kennel building. I led her to the grooming room.

"Get the supplies ready, Mum," I said. "I'll go and get Molly. If anybody can make that mudball look like a million pounds, it's you. You're a pro!"

"Well, thank you, Alfie," Mum said with a smile.

I raced out the front door to find Molly. I was going to make sure I got my twenty pounds!

I finally found her in the garden. I couldn't believe my eyeballs! She'd somehow got into the dogs' playground, behind the kennel building. Molly was busy digging a deep hole in the middle of the park.

"Hey, how did you get in there, girl?" I called. "The gate is locked."

Then I noticed a hole under the fence. It hadn't been there before.

"Wow, Molly," I called. "You're the alpha digger – the speediest around!"

I climbed over the fence and picked her up. "You're even dirtier now," I said. "But that doesn't matter. Mum will clean you up."

I carried her out of the park and through the kennel building. *This is going to be the easiest twenty pounds I've ever earned*, I thought.

Inside, Mum shut the grooming-room door behind us. A quiet, peaceful song played on the MP3 player.

Mum placed a dog brush on the floor. She put a doggie treat beside the brush. I gently placed Molly next to them.

"Yum," I said. "Go and get the tasty treat."

Molly didn't even look at the snack. She stared at the hairbrush and started to cry. She backed into a corner.

I grabbed the brush and said, "It's okay, Molly. Look – it's not sharp or anything." I moved the brush towards her.

Mum said, "Alfie, no."

Too late. Molly started to shiver and cry even louder.

Mum took the brush and dropped it in a drawer. "We can't rush this, Alfie," she said. "Come here, Molly. It's okay."

Mum kneeled down and put a treat on the floor. Molly smelled it. Then, really slowly, she ate it.

"Come here, little one." Mum popped Molly onto her lap. "If you were brushed every day, little girl, it wouldn't be so painful. Your hair is full of knots because you don't let people brush it. That's what makes combing it so painful."

Mum tried to run her fingers through Molly's hair. She leaned over and looked closely at Molly's skin.

"Oh, no," Mum said. "Your skin is sore, Molly. This must be very uncomfortable for you! It must be driving you mad, isn't it? You should be bathed every week, at least. With a dog shampoo for skin problems. Oh, yes, we've got to get you better."

Mum gave Molly another treat. This time Molly wolfed it down.

"Would you at least let me brush your teeth today?" Mum asked her. "If you don't let people brush your teeth, you could become a very poorly little dog. Horrible things could start to happen, even in other parts of your body."

Suddenly I didn't care about the twenty pounds anymore. I just wanted to help Molly get better.

"Can I help?" I asked.

"Yes, please," Mum said. "Grab a dog toothbrush and the dog toothpaste. She'll like the flavour."

At that moment, Alfreeda ran into the grooming room. "Mum!" she said. "Primrose and Harry are back! They're just driving up."

"Oh, I wonder if they've forgotten something," Mum said.

Suddenly Harry came tearing towards us. He popped his head inside the room and looked straight at Molly.

"Oh, good," he said, out of breath. "There she is. Is she wearing the collar?"

"Which collar?" Alfreeda said.

Harry winked at me and said, "You know, Alfie. The special collar?"

"Oh, yes," I said. I kneeled down and felt around Molly's neck. I dug deep under the long, shaggy hair. It was filled with knots and bits of food and dirt.

"Mum," I said. "Did you take off Molly's collar?"

"No." Mum shook her head. "I don't think she was wearing one."

"It's gone!" I cried.

⬥— CHAPTER 7 —⬥
What terriers do best

Harry looked as scared as a rabbit trapped by a terrier. Even his bushy beard trembled.

Primrose ran into the grooming room and stared at him.

"What's going on now, Harry?" she asked. "We should be at the groom's dinner! I'm sure everyone is waiting for us."

Harry took a deep breath and explained everything. He told her about the collar, the rings, the surprise. "But I suppose I didn't put the collar on properly," he said. "It must've fallen off."

Primrose clasped her hand over her mouth.

Suddenly Harry pointed at Alfreeda and me. "As soon as I find my wallet, I'll give twenty pounds to the first person to find those rings!" he said.

"Wow," Alfreeda said and looked at me. "Twenty pounds! Come on! I'll check the driveway." She sprinted towards the front door.

"I know where the collar might be," I said. "Come on, everybody."

I dashed to the playground. Everyone else tore after me.

"Molly has just dug that hole," I said and pointed at the fence. "Maybe the collar dropped into it." Then I pointed towards the middle of the playground. "Molly has just dug that hole too."

"Which one?" Harry asked. "There are so many out here."

"Um, I'm not sure," I said, looking around. Harry was right. There were holes all over the park.

"We've had lots of terriers stay at Hound Hotel recently," Mum said. "They're just doing what terriers do best: dig."

Suddenly Primrose whirled around and said, "Alfie, can we have a rake and a spade please?"

"Follow me," I said.

I led her to the garage. We filled an old red wheel barrow with spades, rakes and piles of gardening tools.

We pushed the wheel barrow all the way to the park. Everyone was on their knees now. Their fingers combed through grass, mud and small rocks. Molly was digging a new hole.

❀ ❀ ❀

Before long, the whole wedding party appeared at Hound Hotel. Primrose had decided to call off the dinner and wedding rehearsal. She wanted everyone to help search for the rings.

The men threw off their smart suit jackets. The women kicked off their high heels. Everybody was busy digging and raking and combing through the soil with their fingers.

"Where could those rings be?" cried Primrose.

Soon more of Harry and Primrose's family and friends turned up to help. Molly and three other Hound Hotel guests helped dig too. Holes and piles of soil covered the playground.

At about eight o'clock, the sun set and then clouds covered the stars. It started to rain. It was just a sprinkle. But it was enough to turn the soil into mud and the helpers into mudballs.

"Let's have a break and get something to eat," said Harry's dad. "We have a car full of sandwiches and lemonade."

After all that digging, everyone was starving. We tucked into the food without even cleaning ourselves up.

The maid of honour sipped her lemonade and yawned. "Maybe we should call it a night," she suggested.

"No!" Primrose cried. "I'm *not* leaving this doggie park until we find those rings!"

Everyone gathered around her. "We'll keep searching, Primrose," said Harry.

"We can even set up some tents for people to rest in," Mum offered.

So Harry and I set up every dog tent we could find in the attic. We made tents out of blankets, too. They covered the farmyard.

Then Harry and I got back to digging. I used every bit of alpha-boy strength I could find. I kept rubbing dirt out of my eyes and thinking, *I'm going to find those wedding rings. Any minute now, I'll be twenty pounds richer.*

We all kept searching until midnight. Then everyone crawled into the tents and fell asleep.

First thing the next morning, we got straight back to it.

⟡— CHAPTER 8 —⟡
A true Westie

Molly wasn't groomed in time for the photos. But no one else was either. Primrose called off the photographer. "We can't have our pictures taken looking like this," she said. "Keep digging!"

So we kept moving piles of soil and grass around and around.

At midday, Primrose's mum begged her to stop the search. "Everyone needs to get ready for the wedding," she said.

"No," said Primrose. "We can't give up yet.

I'm not leaving this park without those rings. We'll just have to have the wedding here!"

Harry took Primrose's hand and asked, "Are you sure? You wanted Molly and I to look perfect, and now no one looks perfect. Well, except you. You always look perfect to me."

"Oh, Harry," Primrose said with a sigh. "I'm sure. Perhaps how we all look isn't as important as I thought. We can still have a wedding filled with love, even if everyone's covered in mud!"

She made some phone calls, and the registrar arrived moments later. Then a couple of florists swept in with roses, ivy and a posh metal stand.

At two o'clock, Harry and Primrose stood in front of the roses, on top of a pile of soil. They faced each other and held hands. Primrose looked like a spring flower in her yellow dress. A mud-splashed one.

The rest of the wedding party lined up in rows. I threw rose petals all over the playground, and Molly chased them. She tried to grab them out of the air, as if they were birds or moths or dragonflies. It was actually really good fun.

When the petals were gone, I stood with my empty basket on one side of the registrar, next to the groom.

Alfreeda stood on the other side of the registrar, next to the bridesmaids. She held a little Hound Hotel doggie pillow. Harry had pinned an IOU to the top. The little piece of paper said:

My dear Primrose,
IOU one wedding ring.
love, Harry

Everyone else sat in the playground, wherever there wasn't a big hole. Nobody had time to get cleaned up. Nobody had done their hair or changed into their smart clothes.

The registrar faced Harry and Primrose. He started to talk about marriage. Suddenly the crowd started oohing and ahhing. People pointed at the rose and ivy display.

I looked up. Two robins sat in the roses, just above Harry's and Primrose's heads. The robins sat side by side, their heads touching.

"Ah," said the registrar. "Love birds."

Suddenly Molly started to bark her head off at the robins. The birds took off, flying towards the chicken coop.

The registrar returned to his speech. But I kept watching the robins. They landed on the chicken coop roof. I noticed a nest up there.

I stared at it. Something sparkled in the bright sunshine. My heart started to beat quickly.

I reached around the registrar and poked Alfreeda. Then I pointed at the nest.

Her eyes grew as big and as round as a Westie's.

In about twenty seconds flat, we dashed out of the playground and over to the garage. We needed a stepladder.

We leaned it against the chicken coop. "I'll do it," I said before Alfreeda had the chance. I scaled the ladder at alpha-boy speed.

Straight away, the robins flew to the other side of the roof. They chirped at me, loud and angry.

"Don't worry," I said. "I won't hurt your babies."

Four things lay at the bottom of the nest: two blue eggs and two gold rings. Very carefully, I took the rings out of the nest. I didn't touch the eggs at all. And I left Molly's collar. It was twisted into the nest, between straw and grass and wildflowers.

"Found them!" I cried. I leapt off the ladder and ran back to the crowd.

Everybody cheered. I gave the rings to Harry. He shook my hand, then Alfreeda's, and cried, "I knew I could count on you kids!"

I looked at my sister. A big grin covered her muddy face.

I grinned back and whispered, "I'm not taking money from a man who keeps losing his wallet."

"Me neither," she whispered. "Who cares anyway? Did you see the size of that cake?"

I nodded. "Oh, yes! I can't wait."

So Harry and Primrose got back to getting married.

Not long after they said, "I do," they cut the cake. Alfreeda and I both had thirds. And Molly had the biggest slice of all. Now she had yellow lemon cake all over her face too.

"We'll clean you up, Moll, old girl," I said.

"Yeah, when Harry and Primrose are on their honeymoon," Alfreeda said. "We'll be really gentle, Molly, you'll see. Before long, being groomed won't be scary anymore. You'll look like a true Westie by the time your mum and dad get back."

Molly barked and wagged her tail.

"Hey," I said. "We should decorate the honeymoon car!"

"Yes!" said Alfreeda. "Come on, Molly. You can help."

In no time at all we had decorated the tiny yellow car. We wrote "JUST MARRIED" on the windows with bars of dog soap. We tied empty dog-food cans onto the back bumper.

Mum took a photograph of the car, with everyone standing around it. The whole messy, muddy wedding party, with Molly right smack in the middle. Her pink tongue hung out of her mouth. And her tail wagged so quickly that it blurred in the picture.

That night, Alfreeda and I taped the picture over the dog-grooming table. It would be our "before grooming" snapshot of Molly.

Then we filled the holes up in the playground.

That is, until Molly dug them up again.

Is a West Highland terrier the dog for you?

Hi! It's me, Alfreeda!

I'm sure you'd love to have your own cute, little, adorable Westie now too, wouldn't you? I don't blame you. Westies are great pets for families! That is, most families. But before you dash out to buy or adopt one, here are some important facts you should know:

Westies are very good at barking. So if you have a little baby at your house who needs to sleep a lot, get a pet rabbit instead. Barking is a Westie's way of saying she's happy or nervous or bored. If you DO get a Westie, don't shout at her when she barks. Shouting just makes dogs bark more! Stay calm and say "no barking" in a quiet voice. Give her a treat when she stops.

Westies LOVE to chase anything that runs away from them: mice, rabbits, squirrels, children. The faster another animal runs away, the faster a Westie will chase it. When this happens, a Westie won't listen to its owner. So Westies HAVE to be on leads or in a fenced-in garden to stay safe when they're outside.

Westies need lots of attention. If they're left alone for too long, they'll get bored and lonely, then they'll bark, dig and chew things. So if you're the kind of family that's always out at work and school and football matches and music lessons, don't get a Westie. Get a goldfish.

Okay, signing off for now ... until the next adventure at Hound Hotel!

Yours very factually,

Alfreeda Wolfe

Glossary

alpha   person or animal who is the leader and is the best or most powerful one in a group

collar   thin band of leather or other material that an animal wears around its neck, often it has information that says who the animal belongs to in case it gets lost

decision   act of making up your mind

honeymoon   holiday that a newly-married couple spend together

kennel   place where dogs are kept and cared for while their owners are away

overboard   doing something with too much excitement and doing more than is needed

registrar   person who can legally perform non-religious weddings

rehearsal   practice for something to make sure everyone knows what to do

shaggy   long, rough, messy hair

suspicious   feeling that something is wrong or bad, even though there's no proof

Talk about it

1. Alfie's mum forced him to get his hair cut to make sure he looked nice for the wedding. Talk about a time when your parents asked you to dress up for an event. Did it make you cross, or did you enjoy dressing up?

2. Think about a wedding you've been to. How was the wedding in the book different from the wedding you attended? How was it the same?

3. On page 68, Alfreeda has shared some facts and opinions about West Highland terriers. Do you think that a Westie would be a good dog for your family? Why or why not?

Write about it

1. Write a letter to the twins' dad, telling him about the crazy wedding. Use either Alfie's or Alfreeda's point of view.

2. Alfie did not want to be the page boy, but in the end, he had fun. Write about a time when your parent made you do something you didn't want to do. Was it as bad as you had imagined it would be?

3. Put together a factsheet about West Highland terriers. Use three or more reputable sources to help you.

About the author

Shelley Swanson Sateren grew up with five pet dogs –
a beagle, a terrier mix, a terrier-poodle mix, a
Weimaraner and a German shorthaired pointer. As an
adult, she has adopted a lively West Highland white
terrier called Max. Apart from writing many children's
books, Shelley has worked as a children's book editor and
in a children's bookshop. She lives in Minnesota, USA,
with her husband, and has two grown-up sons.

About the illustrator

Deborah Melmon has worked as an illustrator for
over 25 years. After graduating from the Academy of
Art University in San Francisco, she began her career
illustrating covers for a weekly magazine supplement
Since then, she has produced artwork for over twenty
children's books. Her artwork can also be found on
wrapping paper, greeting cards and fabric. Deborah
lives in California, USA, and shares her studio with an
energetic Airedale terrier called Mack.

www.raintree.co.uk